Magic
Ball

For Johnny

A. F.

For my magical wife, Amy

M. R.

EGMONT
We bring stories to life

Book Band: Turquoise

Lexile® measure: 570L

First published in Great Britain 2017
by Egmont UK Ltd
The Yellow Building, 1 Nicholas Road, London W11 4AN
Text copyright © Anne Fine 2017
Illustrations copyright © Matt Robertson 2017
The author and illustrator have asserted their moral rights.
ISBN 978 1 4052 8455 4
www.egmont.co.uk
A CIP catalogue record for this title is available from the British Library.
Printed in Singapore.
65228/1

Stay safe online. Any website addresses listed in this book are correct at the time of going
to print. However, Egmont is not responsible for content hosted by third parties. Please
be aware that online content can be subject to change and websites can contain content
that is unsuitable for children. We advise that all children are supervised
when using the internet.

Magic Ball

Anne Fine

Illustrated by Matt Robertson

Reading Ladder

Olly could never make up his mind.

His mum said, 'Do you want to wear the blue or the green shirt?'

Olly had a think. The blue shirt had handy buttons, but the green shirt was easier to tuck in.

'Hurry up, please,' Mum told him.
'Choose, Olly. Blue or green?'

It was so hard. Olly stood trying
to decide, till Mum ran out of time and
pulled the green shirt over his head.

5

It was the same in class. Mrs Banks asked, 'Olly, do you want to paint, or work with clay?'

Clay was more fun. But Sarah was painting, and Olly liked sitting by Sarah because she made him laugh.

'Hurry up and choose!' Mrs Banks said. 'I can't wait all day.' But Olly couldn't choose, so Mrs Banks just steered him to a seat by the clay bin.

When Olly got home, Mum opened the fridge door. 'What snack do you want today? I could make a tuna fish sandwich. Or cheese and crackers. Or open a can of soup.'

Oh, it was impossible! Tuna was lovely. But so were cheese and crackers. Or he could have his favourite soup – tomato. What should he choose?

Olly stood on one leg. He was miserable. He liked his green shirt and his blue shirt. He liked clay and painting. He liked tuna, and cheese and crackers, and tomato soup.

What Olly didn't like was having to *choose*.

On Saturday, Uncle Tyler came to visit. It was pouring with rain. First Uncle Tyler and Olly played Monster Snap. Then they built towers with plastic bricks. Then Uncle Tyler read stories to Olly.

Suddenly the rain stopped.

'Good!' Uncle Tyler said. 'Now we can go out. We could go to the petting zoo. Or to the river to feed the ducks. Or to the play park. You choose, Olly.'

But Olly couldn't choose. He liked
the petting zoo, of course. But he also
loved going to the river to feed the ducks
that fussed around his feet.

Then again, it was always fun to
go to the park, especially with Uncle
Tyler, who pushed the swing higher than
Mum ever did.

'I can't decide!' he said.

'Just choose,' said Uncle Tyler.

'I can't!' wailed Olly. 'I can't
choose. I never can!'

He burst
into tears.

'I know what you need,' Uncle Tyler said. 'We'll go and get one now. Jump in the car.'

Uncle Tyler drove into town. They walked along the High Street till they came to a shop called Pete's Variety Store.

'What's a Variety Store?' asked Olly.

'It's a shop that sells everything,' said Uncle Tyler. 'Odd things you've never come across, and things you didn't even know you wanted till you spot them on the shelves. You wait and see.'

Olly soon saw. The shop was stuffed with all sorts. There were frilly hats and garden gnomes and spectacles with no glass. There were glove puppets and mats to kneel on if you were planting bulbs in the garden.

You could buy a pretend dinosaur tooth, or a tiger mask, or something to make your bedtime milk go frothy.

Suddenly Uncle Tyler pointed. 'Look! **There!**'

He reached up to the top shelf and took down a box. It was purple and shiny and square.

'It's the last one,' he said. 'We're very, very lucky.'

Olly followed Uncle Tyler to the counter. Uncle Tyler paid, and the lady put the box in a bag and gave it to Olly, saying, 'Take care not to drop it.'

'What is it?' Olly asked his uncle. 'What's inside the box?'

'You wait and see,' said Uncle Tyler again.

They got back in the car and drove home.

Olly lifted the box out and looked at it carefully. Four of the six sides were just shiny purple. The fifth side said, *Handle With Care*, and on the sixth in fancy letters it said, Magic Ball.

'Magic Ball?' Olly said. 'What's a magic ball?'

Uncle Tyler grinned. 'It's what you need. Now you won't have to do your own choosing any more. Just ask the magic ball. It chooses for you.'

'How?'

'Take it out and see.'

So Olly opened the box and lifted out the magic ball. Just like the box it came in, it was purple and shiny. At the top was a little window.

'Ask it a question,' said Uncle Tyler.
'I don't know what to ask,' said Olly.

Mum said, 'Ask if we should have pizza for supper.'
So Olly asked the ball, 'Should we have pizza for supper?'
'Roll it over, then look in the window,' said Uncle Tyler.

Olly rolled the ball over and bent
his head to peer in the little window. A
tiny triangle of plastic floated to the top.
There was a message on it: *Good idea*.

'Good idea,' Olly said.

'Fine,' Olly's mother said, and went
to make a salad to go with the pizza.

'Ask it another question,' Uncle Tyler said.

Olly rolled the ball over again, then asked it, 'Will I have to go to bed at my usual time, even though Uncle Tyler is here?'

He waited for a plastic bar to float to the top. This one said, *Yes.*

Olly thought of another question.
'Will I ever get a puppy?'

The ball said, *Ask again later.*

'How does it *work*?' asked Olly.
'How does it know the answers?'

'That is a mystery,' said Uncle
Tyler. 'Perhaps it really is magic.'

All the rest of the day, Olly asked his magic ball about everything.

'Shall I pretend I can't find my homework reading book?' (The ball said, *No*.)

'Will I get a bike for my birthday?' (The ball said, *Don't bet on it*.)

'Should I play on my scooter now?'
(The ball said, *Ask again later*, and when
Olly asked again later, it said, *No*.)

When Uncle Tyler was leaving,
Olly hugged him. 'Thank you for my
present,' he said. 'I love my magic ball.
It makes things so much easier.'

That night, he sat in bed and
turned the ball over and over to find out
how many answers it had. He counted
eight. There was *Yes, No, Ask again later,
Never, Don't bet on it, Good idea, Bad idea*
and *Maybe*.

Next morning was sunny and bright. Mum asked Olly, 'Shall we walk to school today?'

'Just a minute,' said Olly. He rushed back to his bedroom to ask the magic ball.

The ball said *Yes*, so Mum and Olly set off. 'This ball is brilliant!' Olly told her. 'I'll never have to choose for myself again.'

'You wait and see,' his mum warned. 'It's gone well so far. But maybe the day will come when you and the ball don't agree.'

'I don't think so,' said Olly. 'I think I shall use it for ever and ever and ever.'

His mother didn't argue. She just smiled.

All week, Olly made the ball do his choosing for him.

It told him to wear the football pyjamas, not the spotty ones.

It told him he wanted chocolate ice-cream, not raspberry.

It told him to tidy up his room
before supper, not after.

Then on Saturday,
something went wrong.
Mum and Olly
were in the
cafe after
swimming.

Mum always had coffee and a tea
cake. Olly always had chocolate cake.

But while they were waiting in the queue, Olly made the mistake of asking the magic ball, 'Shall I have chocolate cake?' The ball said, *No*.

Quickly, Olly rolled it in his hands and asked the question again.

No, said the ball again.

But Olly always had chocolate cake. It was the only cake in the cafe that he really liked. He asked a third time.

This time the ball said, *Ask me later.*

'I don't have *time*,' wailed Olly because the serving lady was already waiting. 'I'll have a coffee and a tea cake,' said Olly's mother. 'And Olly will have chocolate cake as usual.'

'No, I won't,'
Olly said.
'Not chocolate
cake. Not today.'

'The only other cake is coconut,'
the serving lady told him.

Olly was in a fluster. He wasn't
fond of coconut. But he didn't want to
go against the magic ball. So he just
nodded. 'All right. I'll have that.'

He didn't like it. He ate most of
it, but it was nowhere near as nice as
chocolate cake.

'That's something I won't ask the
magic ball again!' he told his mother.

36

After that, things went very wrong
indeed. The magic ball told him to
pretend he'd cleaned his teeth when
he hadn't, but Mum saw that his
toothbrush was still dry, and told
him off.

It told
    him not
        to bother
            to wear
                his wellies
                    to the park,
                    but that
                    meant he
                    couldn't jump
            in puddles.

It told him to spend the money he
had saved on football cards. But there
were no shinies in the
packs he bought,
and he was
sorry after.

YES

Then it was Sarah's birthday party. 'We'll have to get a present,' Olly's mother said. They went to the shops.

First Olly saw the snapping head of a velociraptor on a stick, but the magic ball told him she wouldn't want it.

Then Olly's mother found a book of poems with wonderful pictures.

'Sarah will like this, won't she?' But the magic ball said, *Never.*

After that, Olly picked out a woolly hat with a pink and blue bobble on top. The magic ball said, *Bad idea.*

'This is ridiculous!' said Olly's mum. 'We're going into one more shop, then home, with or without a present.'

The last shop had the loveliest bright puzzle cube. 'Sarah will love that,' said Olly's mother.

'I have to ask the ball,' said Olly.

'No, you don't,' said Olly's mother. 'That ball is not the boss of you. You can decide for yourself.'

But Olly had asked the ball each time and didn't think that he should stop at the end. He turned it over and asked it, 'Should I buy Sarah that lovely puzzle cube?'

No, said the ball.

Olly burst into tears. His mother took his hand. 'We're going home right now.'

'But I haven't got a present for Sarah's party!' wailed Olly.

'You can blame the magic ball for that,' said Olly's mum.

Olly didn't just blame it. He got rid
of it. He wrapped it in bright silver tissue,
and put it back in its shiny purple box.
He wrapped the box with fancy paper
and ribbon.

He wrote a label.

Happy birthday, Sarah.
This ball isn't real magic. It's just fun.

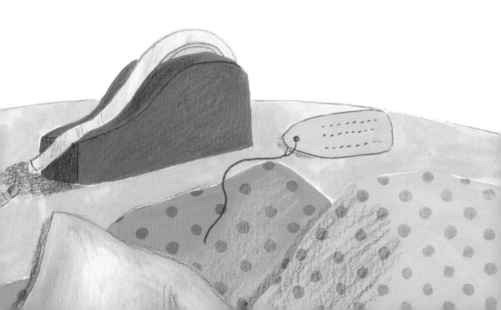

It was a splendid party. Sarah *adored* the ball. Everyone sat round it, asking stupid questions and getting stupid answers. It was the best present ever.

Next morning, Olly's mother asked him, 'Which shirt today? Is the red one OK?'

Olly thought that the ball would probably have told him, *Yes*.

So he said very firmly, 'No. I choose the green.'